Tal

GW00863586

of the

London Boulevardier

Volume 6

Random Acts of Mass Hysteria in

The Graffiti Zone

Francis Charlton

Best Wishes

Francis

Tales

of the

London Boulevardier

Volume 6

Random Acts of Mass Hysteria in

The Graffiti Zone

Francis Charlton

For

Eloise

Thanx to Rod Serling for the

Twilight Zone opening narratives

And to HG Wells and Jeff Wayne

Introduction

Respectfully submitted for your approval, Portrait of an Artist. The time the early 21st century, the place: London. The man on the pavement, the artist in question Dave, also known as The London Boulevardier. He loves London Town. This is his city, it is his inspiration. He is a successful painter of women and a chronicler of contemporary culture. He is an essential guest to invite to an opening, he provides cache, style and a satiric wit, which many believe he acquired in The Graffiti Zone.

6

Preface

It was a time of madness

of masterminds, madmen and murderers

of genocide, homicide and suicide

of narcissism, self-interest and self-promotion

It was a time of insanity

It was a time to post it and wait for the reaction

Thus arose a New Age.

The age of *The Selfie*

Hell.No!

If you only read one magazine this month

It must be **Hell.No!**

Hell Yes! It's **Hell.No! Magazine**

Pictures with no words

For *Generation Selfie*

Forget Facebook, Instagram and Twitter

It's **Hell.No! Online**

First with celebrity death flash footage.

One

'To the average person, an art gallery is a place of beauty and colour and wonder. Some people come to seek inspiration, others to contemplate paintings, others to look for the sheer joy of looking. Derek Meadows has his own reasons. He comes to the gallery to get away from the world. It isn't really the Espresso Bar which has drawn him here everyday, it's the fact that here in these rooms he can be alone for a little while, really and truly alone. Anyway that's how it was before he got lost and wandered into the room that was not even a footnote in his programme, for this room was in the Graffiti Zone.

They never found Derek Meadows, because the curator didn't tell them what he saw on the wall. He knew what they'd say, and he knew they'd be right, too, because seeing is not always believing, especially if what you see happens to be sprayed on the wall of the Graffiti Zone.'

'... I've been having a terrible dream, an apocalyptic dream, a dream of a world in turmoil.'

'Just what is this dream, Dave?'

'It's the American Dream!'

'Thanks Dave for agreeing to record a *'Boulevardier about Town'* segment for the programme. Where shall we start?'

'Mariela.'

'Dave.'

'Mariel.'

'Yes Dave?'

'I've already started.'

'Started what?'

'The interview, channeling Rod Serling as a cultural reference.

'Er!'

'Mariela, it may be time for a nice cup of tea.'

'Er...what are we talking about?'

'This is becoming frightfully tiresome.'

'Clive.'

'Dave.'

'The studio floor is yours…'

'Thanx Dave. I suggest that he's beyond comedy.'

'Wassa matter you?' Says Vincenzo.

'There is nothing about the man that is remotely funny,' replies

Clive.

'Gotta show respect,' says Vincenzo, pointing at Clive.

'He's beyond parody,' says Wanksta©.

'I fucka your momma,' says Vincenzo looking at Colin 45©.

'Beyond satire,' says Nine Mil Phil©.

'I make him an offer he cannot refuse,' says Vincenzo.

'Interesting!' I say, however, this getting us nowhere!'

'Perhaps,' says Steve, 'we're in a state of Mass Hysteria, but no one recognises the signs!'

'Mamma Mia!' Exclaims Vincenzo.

'You may be onto something,' I say.

'Mother of Mercy?' Declares Vincenzo.

'We'll call our next exhibition 'Random Acts of Mass Hysteria©.

'Love it Dave, the first joint…'

'...collaboration between Dave, the London Boulevardier and Wanksta©, and Steve McCracken NONEHERE. It'll be Warhol and Basquiat and er...someone else, all over again,' suggests Colin 45©.

'Ali, Frazier and er...Ali's ego,' contributes Clive.

'Smith and Wesson and the guy who pulls the trigger,' says Nine Mil Phil©.

'That's amore!' Vincenzo sings

'What is?' Asks Clive.

Vincenzo drops to one knee, holds out his arms and sings, *Just one Cornetto. Give it to me. Delicious ice cream. From Italy.* Getting up he points to Colin 45©, saying, 'I go now!'

Colin 45© makes the mistake of asking, 'Going where?'

'To fucka your momma. She is begging me for it. Ciao.'

'And that rounds off the interview,' breathes Mariella, 'although I don't think any of it will air. Thanks for coming to the studio with the Usual Suspects and contributing to the debate on the influence of the arts on the political agenda.'

'It was, and is, and will continue to be my pleasure,' I say, unscrewing the cap from a bottle of Absolut and swallowing half the contents in one gulp. 'Courtesy of the Soho Hotel, I say. 'Mariella?'

'Yes Dave.'

'Mariella.'

'Dave.''

'Mariella would you care to join me for eight or nine pints of London Pride?'

'You do realise, don't you Dave, that it's only 10.15am.'

'Yes Mariella. Yes indeed, I realise that the day is running away from me.'

'Why do you say that Dave?'

'A good question, well asked,' I say.

'And..?'

'And what Mariella?'

'Why is the day running away from you?'

'Because Mariella...' I pause.

'Dave?'

'You want to run away with me?'

'No Dave. I was enquiringly why you thought the day was running away from you?'

'Ah! I see,' I say.

'And?'

'And what?'

'The day?'

'Ah! The day. So much to do and so little time.'

'For what?'

'To arrange the homecoming of the newly weds.'

'Alan the Found Sculpture artist and arts reporter Ms Metro.'

'Yes Mariella. Yes indeed!'

'Where did they honeymoon?'

'Thamesmead, SE11.'

'Why?'

'They don't like to leave London, and they hadn't been to that area, they had, in fact been no further than Woolwich. So they were looking forward to taking in the sights.'

'Sights?'

'The thing honeymooners do. Visit places, take photographs.'

'I've lived here long enough to know there's little of interest in Thamesmead.'

'Mariella .'

'Dave.'

'Mariella.'

'Dave.'

'Mariella .'

'Yes Dave?'

'May I suggest that you're being a little too intellectual about this.'

'Sweet Mother of Mercy!' Exclaims Vincenzo.

'A little too precious!' Suggests Clive.

'Jesus, Mary and Joseph,' continues Vincenzo.

'A little too Radio 4,' says Wanksta©.

'May the Lord have mercy on our souls,' Vincenzo genuflects.'

'For your information my dear, dear Mariella.

'Yes Dave.'

'Dear, dear Mariella.'

'Get to the point Dave!'

'I will, most certainly I will.'

'Sweet Jesus!' Exclaims Vincenzo.

'Well,' I say, 'to continue...Thamesmead is one of those areas that is often slagged off by the cultural élitists, Radio 4 bleatists, and black cab *'I'm not going there defeatists.'* However, there is much of cultural interest associated with the area. This is where you say, *'Really Dave!'*

'Really Dave!'

'Yes Mariella, sociologically speaking, Thamesmead, as you don't know, was developed and built by the Greater London Council as an innovative housing project based on the Swedish model of social housing. It was not a complete success but a brave attempt nonetheless. And this is where you say, *'Do continue Dave.'*

'Dave.'

'Mariella.'

'Pray continue.'

'Thank you. No really, thank you. No really...'

'We're not do this Dave, this is Radio 4 we take what we do seriously.'

'Moving on Mariella, the project was designed around futuristic ideas with a central lake. Thamesmead attracted the creative community seduced by its ambience. Stanley Kubrick set many of the scenes from *'A Clockwork Orange'* in south Thamesmead which included Southmere Lake. The film *'The Optimists of Nine Elms,'* starring Peter Sellers was filmed there. The television drama *'The Misfits,'* and *'My Beautiful Laundrette,'* Channel 4s gay coming of age film were shot there. Don't stop me when I'm on a roll, *'The Firm,'* starring Gary Oldman was filmed there, as was the video *'Come to Daddy,'* by Aphex Twin and directed by Chris Cunningham.'

'Why Dave didn't we start the programme with this?

'You didn't ask Mariella.'

'Holy Mother of God!' Cries Vincenzo prostrating himself over the sound desk.

'I require a pint or two of London Pride, would you, Mariella, care to join us on a trip to oblivion?'

'I don't think so, it sounds a little too final for me?'

'I think you misinterpret my suggestion Mariella.'

'?!??'

'Oblivion, is the name of the new Arts Club in Soho, uniquely it doesn't have a door policy.'

'Why not.'

'It doesn't have a door.'

'How do you get in?'

'Up a ladder and through the second floor window.'

'Perhaps another time Dave.'

'You don't like heights?'

'Not lofty enough for you?' Suggests Wanksta©.

'You expected something less elevated?' I say.

'Glory, glory, Hallelujah.' Vincenzo rather dynamically states.

'More highbrow?' Queries Colin 45©.

'Knock, knock, knocking on Heaven's door!' sings Vincenzo.

'Anyway,' says Steve, 'I'll see you guys later, there are walls that require birds, multi-coloured birds, birds with exotic plumage, birds with...'

'What is he talking about?' asks Mariella, looking not a little perplexed.'

'Fuck knows,' I say, 'I've no idea what I'm talking about most of the time.'

'I love the smell of spray can propellant in the morning,' says Steve.'

'What's the soundtrack?' Asks Wanksta©.

'Anthems for Doom Youth,' replies Steve.

'Going up to the spirit in the sky...' sings Vincenzo.

Mariella staring into a monitor, says, 'Guys there's breaking news reporting that Deviant Vivika Productions are planning a concert in Hyde Park starring the well known, I think that should read 'Well despised' war criminal, despot and stand-up comedian Vlad Smythz in *'It'll be all Reich on the Night.'*

Crowding around the monitor we watch as Sky News reporter Tim monsters Vlad at Heathrow.

'This is going to be entertaining,' I say.

'Who do you think you are?' Says a visibly shaking Tim.

'I am he whom men speak of in hushed tones,' replies Vlad clicking his heels.

Tim, finger on his ear, says, 'I am calm!!'

Vlad continues, 'I bring stand-up satirical observations to you, the culturally clueless.'

Tim, for all his protestations, loses it, 'You're fucking insane!'

Vlad putting a finger to his lips, ponders for a moment and says, 'Let us not forget my Human Rights.'

As Tim lunges at Vlad's throat a sound engineer manhandles him to the ground, 'Take it easy Tim, he's not worth it.'

Tim taking a deep breath, says, 'I think the mindfulness workshop is paying off,' and getting up, he brushes himself down and calmly asks, 'Mr Smythz, please continue, what do you hope to achieve with this tour?'

'You require an explanation, a rationale, perhaps a thesis? Do you think I invade your country to provide you with a soundbite. Is it a *Raison d'être* you require? You would prefer a manifesto?'

Tim has started shaking, clenching his fists until his knuckles turn white.

'I take it that your silence indicates a lack of understanding. You want I paint you a picture using puppets you Guardian reading muppet!'

Tim can just be heard saying, 'I'm cool...'

'My new Reich will be a master-race of stand-up comedians, we have the seal of approval from the most despotic leader of the so-called free world.'

'Don't ask!' I say out loud.

'Too late,' says Mariella.

'Who do you refer to,' queries Tim.

'President Trump.'

Tim leaps into the air, with an ease that suggests he'd been training for this very moment, and before the crew can intervene, scissor kicks Vlad over a trolley of suitcases and onto the luggage carousel, where he goes round and round before being pulled off by airport security.

Tim, meanwhile, is being restrained by anti-terrorist officers, airport security, plain-clothes Old Bill and his own crew. And just before the live feed is cut he can be heard shouting, 'Let me at that motherfucker. He's mine. Say your prayers, you fucking megalomaniacal cu...'

Getting up, I say, I need the bathroom…'

'Dave?'

'Mariella.'

'Dave.'

'I always think,' I say, 'that it's helpful to have been declared insane before agreeing to talk arty bollocks on the radio.'

Reaching the street which reeked of terminal psychosis and self-congratulatory suffocation, I say to Wanksta©, 'I feel the need…'

'…to paint a wall?'

'Yes Wanksta©,' I say, 'Yes indeed.'

'Where are you thinking?'

'SW11,' I say, 'we'll enlist Steve and Vincenzo can be the lookout for us. We require alcohol, much alcohol, let us repair to The Rake we have much to discuss, I may have to cancel my evening of flower arranging.'

Two

Hawthorn Crescent, Battersea SW11. Early summer. A tree-lined enclave of well-to-do residences, there is the residual aromas of barbecues and the laughter of children and the arrival of one or two late home-comers who decided to break their commute with a quiet drink before getting on the Underground. At the sound of the can being shaken and the flashes of colour, it will be precisely 8.52pm on Hawthorn Crescent. This is Hawthorn Crescent on a late Friday evening in Summer. Hawthorn Crescent in the last calm and reflective moment before the street artists came. There's a signpost up ahead - your next stop, the Graffiti Zone .

'Well,' I say to the bar geezer, 'my good friend Steve here will have two bottles of your finest German red, both uncorked no glass required.' Pointing to Wanksta© who, in turn, points at me, I say, 'We will have four pairs of pints of Erdinger, and one packet of dry roasted peanuts. One has to keep up appearances, you know.'

The bar geezer swallows, he's been here before, 'Yes Mr Boulevardier.'

'No need for formalities,' I say, call me Dave. Oh! I nearly forgot, my Italian friend Vincenzo, he of the dubious and quite frankly, dodgy accent, will have one glass of everything *red* from your shelves, one glass of everything *yellow* and two glasses of everything *blue*. In 90 minutes, when he turns green, put him into a black cab and inform the cabbie to deposit him at St. Thomas'. Put the fare and a large tip on my account.'

'Grazia,' says Vincenzo, 'I now drinka the rainbow.'

Commandeering a table, I take out a drawing pad, a 0.4 Rotring and say, 'Where's my Goddamn drinks, I have a campaign to organise. I'm thinking *Universal...*'

'*...Monsters,*' interrupts a smiling Wanksta©.

'People with flaming torches and birds,' says Steve, 'there must be birds.'

'Flaming birds,' suggests Wanksta©.

'You read my mind. I'm thinking flaming birds flying, diving and crashing,' says Steve grinning a grin. The Antithesis of the white dove of peace!'

'Yes indeed,' I say.

'Did you know,' says Steve, 'that the UN symbol, the White Dove of was designed by Picasso?'

Faintly in the background, Vincenzo can just be heard singing, *'Red and yellow and blue and green, I can spew a rainbow, spew a rainblaughhh!'*

'That is an amazing pattern, early period Damien Hirst, I would suggest, says Steve.'

'Moving on,' I say, as Vincenzo is poured into a black cab. 'We hit Battersea with a series of eyeball pleasers, ball tightening squeezers and political teasers. In our first, *'Random Act of Mass Hysteria©*, Battersea will be our canvas and Frankenstein's monster, Dracula and Donald Trump will be our cultural references.'

'Yep!' Says Steve.

'You only have to look at what's happening in Sweden,' says Wanksta©.

Signalling to the bar geezer, I wave my hands over the table of empties and say, 'The same again and the same again with the same again as chasers.' 90 minutes later we flop into a black cab, 'I don't think Vincenzo is going to join us tonight,' I slur.

'Who's Vincenzo?' Queries Wanksta©.

'Your best friend and lookout,' I say.

'Oh yeah!' Says Wanksta©.

'Who are you? AND. Why are there four of you?' Steve asks rubbing his eyes.'

'To cause confusion,' I say.

'They seek him here, they seek him there,' sings Wanksta©.

'The Kinks.' Says Steve, 'Which reminds me...'

'Reminds you...' I say.

'Yes, reminds me.'

'Reminds you of what Steve?'

'I don't know. I appear to have forgotten. Could you remind me?'

'Remind you of what?'

'What I've forgotten?'

'What have you forgotten?'

'I don't know Dave, I think I've forgotten.'

'Perhaps you need reminding.'

'Reminding of what?'

'I've no idea.'

'Anyway Dave, the Kinks.'

'Yes Steve.'

'It reminds me.'

'Yes.'

'When does Ivanka return from Moscow?'

'Tomorrow.'

'What are we talking about?' Asks Wanksta©.

'I have no idea, and I care even less, it's all becoming frightfully tiresome.'

'Dave.'

'Frightfully tiresome,' I repeat.

'Dave?'

'Dave?'

Three

Portrait of The Boulevardier, who acts and thereby gets things done. Dave the Boulevardier might be called a prime mover, a talent which has to be seen to be believed. In just a moment, he'll show his friends how he keeps both feel on the ground and his head in the Graffiti Zone.

'Dave! Dave. Is your name Dave?'

Opening my eyes I look up at three Old Bill staring down at me, 'Why do you ask?'

'I'm asking the questions,' says Old Bill #2, ' and, further to my colleagues initial question, are those two males under the bench you're reclining on friends of yours?'

Looking through the bench slats I can see Wanksta© and Steve cuddling and snoring very loudly. 'I don't recognise them. Who are they?'

'Can I make it clear, that we are the ones asking the question, says Old Bill #2, which leads me to ask, can you account for your whereabouts between midnight and 3am today?'

'That's a good question,' says Old Bill #1.

'I concur,' says Old Bill #3.

'Well can you?' Demands Old Bill #2 fingering a can of pepper spray.

'Can I what?'

'That's what is commonly called a question,' says Old Bill #2, 'and you do not ask them, it is we who ask the questions.'

'Let me go on record and state that this conversation has reached new depths of tedium,' I say, and put my feet up on the bench.

'We ask...'

'Carl?'

'Yes.'

'I don't think that was a question,' says Old Bill #1.

'What was it then?'

'More of a statement, he was expressing his personal opinion.'

Carl scratches his helmet. 'Okay then. Let me explain, we, the Police, ask the questions and you provide us with answers to said questions.'

'Why?'

'That was a question,' says Carl.

'More of a query,' says Old Bill #3.

'Or, perhaps an inquiry, ' says Old Bill #1

'Can I make a statement?' I ask.

'No.' Says Carl.

'Why not?'

'Reasonable response,' says Old Bill #3.

'You are required to be under arrest to make a statement, and currently you are a person of interest in an alleged graffiti incident. We require information.'

'What for?'

'To ascertain the identity of the perpetrators.'

'You won't get it.'

'By hook or by crook, we will.'

'Who are you?'

'The Old Bill. And you are helping the us with our inquiries.'

'I will not. I will remain stumm. I will not be described as a graffiti artist, or local artist. I am Dave the London Boulevardier. My art is my own!'

Carl again scratches his helmet, looking at Old Bill #1 and #3 he says, 'I thought we were in control here, this Boulevardier bloke he's asking questions, making statements...'

'Mr Boulevardier,' says a voice from under the bench.

'My God,' I say to the Old Bill, 'I'm hearing voices!'

'Mr Boulevardier,' says another voice.

'I, also, can hear it,' says Old Bill #3, it's as if God was speaking to him.'

'Perhaps God is using him as a conduit, to spread the word,' says Old Bill #1.

'What word? Demands Carl.

'The Word,' says Old Bill #3.

'What fucking word?'

'Carl, calm yourself, we may be in the presence of something divine.'

Wanksta© and Steve crawl from under the bench, 'Mr Boulevardier,' they utter in stereo.

'His disciples have risen,' cries Old Bill #1.

'Praise the Boulevardier,' shouts Old Bill #3.

'This is fucking Monty Python, you pair of fucking halfwits.'

'No need to get upset, councils Old Bill #1.

'He doubts,' says Old Bill #3 shaking his head.'

'What is the 'Word', Wanksta© and Steve ask!'

'Yes tell us,' say Old Bill #1+3.

'You're a pair of fucking plods,' spits Carl pointing at his two colleagues.

Raising my hand for silence, I say, 'He who shall be now known as *'Carl the Cop,'* in a Random Act of Mass Hysteria has questioned The Boulevardier.'

'We ask the questions,' shouts Carl the Cop.

Smacking my lips, I say, 'The Word is *'Breakfast.'* And, I and my two disciples require escorted egress from these private gardens to the local Patisserie Valerie, I believe breakfast is in order.'

Carl the Cop slumps on the now vacated bench, head in hands muttering a liturgy of profanities.

'I don't think he's praying,' comments Steve.

'He asks too many questions,' says Old Bill #3.

'And he does not believe,' says Old Bill #1.

'What doesn't he believe?' Enquires Wanksta©.

'The answers,' says Old Bill #3, he believes everybody's guilty.'

'We're all guilty of something,' I say.

'You are profound in your utterings,' says Old Bill #1.

'Where can we take you,' inquires Old Bill #3.

'Old Compton Street,' I say.

'We will gladly take you in our fast response vehicle. Carl we'll return to collect you, take the time to consider your brush with divinity.'

'You're right there,' says Old Bill #3, 'why would these three honest human beings be up to no good?'

'Indeed,' says Old Bill #1.

'Fucking idiots,' says Carl shaking his head.

'With the siren sounding out a call to 'Get the fuck out of our way,' we run every red light from Chelsea Gardens to Old Compton Street.

'That,' says Old Bill #1, ' is a new record .'

'We had help,' says Old Bill #3.

'Praise be The Boulevardier,' proclaims Steve.

'I'm inclined to agree,' says Wanksta©.

'I and these two, er...disciples, thank you,' I say shaking hands, 'I don't know your names?'

I'm Bill,' says Old Bill #1.

'And I'm...'

'Please,' I say, 'let me guess. 'It's Ben.'

'You are omniscient,' Old Bill Bill cries out.

We wave them goodbye and with much smacking of lips enter Patisserie Valerie. 'We come to worship at your displays of cakes, I say, a table for three, six espresso doppios, six cappuccinos, and twelve brioche please and whatever these guys want.'

Four

Meet Mr AGD, art critic and bouffant at large, on his way to an artists's reception. If he knew what was in store for him he probably wouldn't go, because before this event is over, the artist in residence is going to paste-up AGDs face on every available wall in the West End, the man, the bouffant, with some effects that could only happen in the Graffiti Zone.

'Alan and Ms Metro are meeting us around the corner in the Carlisle for drinks,' I say, wiping brioche crumbs off my chin.

'What time?' Steve asks, spraying the table with a mixture of partially chewed espresso soaked croissant.

'Enjoying your breakfast?' Wanksta© asks, brushing himself down.

'Yes thanx,' says Steve oblivious to the sarcasm and re-coating Wanksta©

'Say nothing in reply,' I say to Wanksta©, 'you're beginning to resemble a Garibaldi biscuit. In answer to your question Steve...' At that very moment my 'phone begins to vibrate and sings out, '...*champagne supernova, champagne super...*' Opening the flip I say, '*You gotta roll with it, you gotta take your time, you gotta say what you say...*'

'Say Dave.'

'Yo! Alan.'

'Dave.'

'Alan.'

'Dave! We're here, your near and there's plenty of beer.'

'On our way,' I say giving the waitress *'The moving finger having writ,'* gesture.

'Aren't you Dave, The Boulevardier, she asks, handing me the bill.

'Yes. And you are?'

'CC.'

'Upper or lower case?'

'Either, I'm well endowed in both cases.'

CC drops her pen with an, 'Oops!' She then turns around and bending at the waist picks it up.

'Coco de Mer? I ask.

'You are good.'

'And are you...'

'...bad? Incorrigible. I require chastisement. Is it true you spank your models...'

'...before I paint them. Yes. Yes indeed.'

'When can I model for you?'

Handing her my card, I say, ' Bell me.'

'I will, and you should know my Coco de Mer panties are very tight, it may take you quite a while to spank them off.'

'It will be my pleasure,' I say.

'And mine.'

'Dave!'

'Wanksta©.'

'Dave.'

'Steve.'

'Dave.'

'Wanksta©.'

'Dave we need to go, Alan's waiting and Nine Mil Phil's© exhibition opens this evening, we don't want to be late.'

'Verily,' I say, 'let us away.'

'Dave.'

'Alan.'

'Dave.'

'Ms Metro.'

'How was the honeymoon?'

'Alan's inspired,' says Ms Metro.

'How so,' asks Steve.

'A good question, well asked,' says Alan.'

'Well?'

'Well what Steve?'

'How as it inspired you?'

'How has what inspired me?'

'Your honeymoon.'

'Why do you ask?'

'Because Ms Metro informed us that your honeymoon has inspired you.'

'Yes Steve, it has?'

'What has?'

'The honeymoon?"

'The honeymoon what Alan.'

'It has inspired me.'

Wanksta©and I look at each other. 'We require more alcohol,' I say, 'much more.'

'Agreed and noted,' confirms Wanksta© walking to the bar. Six pints of London Pride for me, six pints of Pride for him, six pints of Pride chasers for me and six pints of Pride chasers for him.'

The bar guy, pauses for a beat, and asks, 'You want 24 pints of London Pride?'

'You my barkeep friend are good. Although I fail to see the London Pride in front of me.'

'We have an hour before the opening,' I say.

'In that case,' says Wanksta©, make that 48 pints of London Pride.

The bar guy nods.

'And,' I say.

'Yes,' says the bar guy.

'A packet of pork scratchings, one has to keep up appearances, you know.'

'You, Mr Boulevardier, are so sophisticated,' Ms Metro comments, 'which is why Alan and myself would like you to accept the responsibility of being *'Godfather'* to our forthcoming child.'

'I,' I say, 'accept. However, why not, *'Scarface'* to the child?'

'Godfather is traditional,' says Ms Metro.

'Brando or Pacino?'

'Pacino, Dave.'

'HOOAH'! I exclaim.

Arriving at the No! Gallery in Soho, we pour out of the black cab onto the pavement, looking up, I notice AGD looking down at us. Rolling over, I say to Steve, 'AGDs on stilts, is this a circus or a gallery?'

'It's always a circus where you're concerned Dave,' AGD sneers, brushing his fringe out of his eyes.'

'I don't think he likes you.' Says Steve.

'I require a chain saw, I'm going to cut him down to size!'

'Easy Dave,' says Wanksta©, 'if you get up you'll be the same height as him.'

Getting to my knees, I use AGD as a support as I climb up his body. Reaching his lapels, I grab them tightly, pull him towards me and head butt the fucker. He hits the pavement and the claret begins to flow.

'Outstanding,' exclaims Nine Mil Phil©.

'He was saying begging for it,' comments Vincenzo.

The queue waiting to enter the gallery spontaneously applauds, amid shouts of, 'You the Man!'

'Who shouted that?' I ask.

'You did Dave,' says Alan.

Thinking for a moment, I say, 'Yes, I did. Yes indeed,' and air punch the sky.

'That I can use,' says Nine Mil Phil©.

'Dave.'

'Steve?'

'Dave.'

'Steve.'

'Dave, AGD is lying at your feet!'

Now I remember.

AGD looks up at me and croaks, 'My bouffant! What have you done to my bouffant?'

The crowd who had surrounded us, and had been quietly murmuring, *'Finish him! Finish him!'* Began to chant, *'String him up by his fringe. Hang the fucker! Hang the fucker!'*

AGD crawled to his feet with the aid of street furniture, which had been strategically placed to stop white vans parking on the pavement, at that moment a white van filled with Old Bill screeches to a halt on the pavement, repositioning the said furniture into the middle of the road.

The doors are throw open and heavily tooled-up anti-riot officers pour out and start to beat their shields with truncheons. Thinking, 'This beat is infectious,' I start to dance on the spot. The chant grows louder and the truncheon beat becomes one with it, 'Hang the fucker! Hang the fucker! Hang. Hang. Hang.' The crowd also start to dance.

AGD, meanwhile is being questioned by the Old Bill. 'Could you tell me what happened Sir?'

AGD flicks his hair back, checks it in the window of the police van and says, 'that man Dave did smite me!'

The Old Bill touches AGD on the elbow for reassurance and asks, 'Why did you say that?'

'I have no idea, it sounds a little Biblical to me, maybe I have concussion.'

'Do you realise Sir that many people, my colleagues included, have come to regard this man as the second coming?'

'He's always coming, that's what he's known for! Christ Almighty I'm the victim here.'

'I suggest, Sir, that you refrain from taking the Lord's name in vain.'

AGD who has been flicking his hair every-which-way can't resist saying to the Officer's colleague,'I believe your colleague here may be deluded.'

The two Old Bill look at each other, scratch their helmets, and say, 'Sir, we may arrest you for the potential commission of a Hate Crime, so we suggest, that in your own best interests, you remove yourself from this vicinity.'

AGD takes out his phone, speed dials Trevor Sorbie, declares a bouffant emergency, orders an Uber cab and staggering *to* the gutter and looks down.

'Symbolic?' Queries Wanksta©.

'You know,' I say, 'whether it's standing in a gallery in Southhampton or a gallery in Holland or France, it's critics like AGD who never give you a chance, putting on these shows, you know how hard it can be, sometimes, I think, they're going to crucify me!' My phone starts to vibrate and as I pull it from my pocket, it starts to sing, *'All we are saying, is Give is Peace a Chance.'* The chanting crowd takes up the refrain.

'Get me a wardrobe door,' says Colin 45©.

Opening the flip, I say,'Talk to me Yoko!'

'John, it's me Ivanka, we Moscow girls are hip.'

'Where are you?' I ask.

'In a cab, comrade.'

'You're back?'

'Back comrade?'

'Back in the USSR.'

'No comrade, on the Westway, I'll see you later, Da?'

'Yes indeed,' I say, 'yes indeed, most certainly.' Turning to Steve, I say, 'Let us repair to the bar, drink vast quantities and peruse the show.'

Five

Submitted for your approval, one Julien Wh'tever, a slightly worse for wear hairdresser, whose life has been as drab and undistinguished as a bundle of used salon towels. And, though it's very late in his day, he has an errant wish to leave his previous life behind, from *'Scissors,'* *'Snips,'* *'Barnets,'* and *'Hair Today,'* and work in the West End, this is a gift to hImself. Mr Julien Wh'tever, hair cutter, who is soon to discover he is cutting above his ability – said lesson to be learned in the Graffiti Zone.

AGD was lost in the moment, looking at his reflection in the gutter water, as the Uber cab turns the corner at some speed and pulling up alongside him showers him with dirty puddle water, fast food packaging, used condoms and McDonalds scratch cards.

Who, if I may take a moment to interrupt the narrative, wants to win another Big Mac, having just eaten one of those cardboard tasting fuckers? I digress.

The Uber cab hits the remaining street furniture, relocating it to the middle of the road where it lands on top of the previous deposit, creating a spontaneous sculpture. Alan recognising the irony, says, ' I'm having that found sculpture,' and turning to Vincenzo says, 'Can you drive?'

'Vincenzo nods, ' No! I no drive!'

'Even better,' says Alan throwing his keys to Vincenzo. 'It's the White Transit parked on the double yellow lines. I'll act as a distraction, while you load the van.'

'By your command,' says Vincenzo slapping his chest.

Meanwhile AGD has been escorted by two stylist into the back of the Uber cab, tapping the driver on the shoulder, he says, 'I am AGD, the renowned art critic, and my coiffure is in urgent need of attention!' The two stylists sitting either side of him, are brushing his shoulders and lapels having noticed a sprinkling of dandruff. The Uber driver, who speaks no English, grunts.

I'll spell it out for you,' sighs AGD. 'Take me to Trevor's salon in Covent Garden, my coiffure requires resurrection, and make it fast.'

The driver who had learned his, so-called, skills driving a flatbed and dodging Hellfire missiles in Kandahar, and had subsequently honed these skills driving a yellow cab in New York, grunts, slams it into gear, saying, 'Point! Direction!'

AGD points straight ahead, saying, 'Drive, until I say stop!'

AGD and the two stylists are thrown back into their seats as the cab, reaching speeds of up to 90mph and ignoring No Entry/One Way signs heads toward Covent Garden.

Two high speed police pursuit vehicles give chase to the Uber Cab.

The Uber driver, a little panicked, shoves his head out the window, points and shouts, *'The alley, at back!'* And drives straight down it. Members of the public mishearing him call the Anti-Terrorism Hotline, resulting in three vehicles of heavily armed police, and a short prop helicopter full of SAS personnel to join the pursuit.

The cab driver noticing the helicopter, loses it and screams, 'Hellfire! I give you Hellfire,' through his window. Again the Hotline is flooded by the vigilant public this time resulting in two matt-black FWD Mercedes filled with black mesh balaclava wearing SAS soldiers to interdict with the Uber cab.

AGD recognising that they are boxed-in between Drury Lane and Bow Street, whispers to the driver, 'Put this on Trevor's account, we'll walk the rest of the way.' Taking the hands of the two stylists, he surreptitiously slips out of the cab and walks up Cecil Court to Floral Street

Meanwhile, two SAS soldiers have dropped from the helicopter onto the roof of the cab, popped two flash-bang grenades through the drivers and passengers windows, and as they're winched back into the chopper, eight armed anti-terrorist police storm the cab, while the ground force SAS team watch the rooftops.

AGD, stopping only once to check his hair in the window of the Camper store, pushes the stylists out of his way, throws himself through the open door of the salon, and, falling to his knees, throws his arms up to the heavens and exclaims, 'Trevor!' My coiffure requires assistance!'

He is approached by the receptionist who helps him to his feet. 'Mr AGD, Trevor sends his apologies, unfortunately he cannot be here himself to attend to your, er, coiffure. However, our new stylist, Julien

Wh'tever will tend to your, um, coiffure requirements. Sitting AGD in a chair, she walks back to reception swallowing a giggle and making a hand gesture of cutting her throat, whispering, 'Don't laugh,' to the other stylists.

AGD takes the opportunity to flick his hair in the mirror in front of him. Refocusing, he is suddenly aware of someone standing behind him.

'Mr AGD,' says the figure, 'I'm Julian Wh'tever your stylist. How can I be of hair service to you?'

'I require an intensive hair care experience, to restore my coiffure to its usual elegant, understated, but profound presence on my head.'

'I maybe the stylist you are looking for, I studied with Vidal.'

'Sassoon?'

'No. Vidal Ridal at his hairdressers in Chelmsford.'

'Really,' says AGD, staring at Julian in the mirror. 'Where else?'

'Di put me touch with John Frieda.'

'Princess Di?'

'No. Di the sheep shearer, from Aberystwyth.'

Glancing at his watch, AGD says, 'In two hours I'm on the panel of BBC 2s weekly roundup of the Arts. Mariella wants to interview me on the phenomenon of the, so-called, street artists showing in the major galleries.'

'I suggest you get on with it, while I have a power nap, a cab will collect me in 90 minutes.'

Julien, *'Snip, snips,'* his scissors behind AGD, 'This will make my career,' he thinks.

AGDs eyes close, 'After the day I've had,' he thinks, 'I deserve a little me time,' and promptly falls asleep.

Six

Portrait of a nervous man. AGD by name, art critic by profession. A man beset by life's problems, his job, his salary, the competition to get ahead, and especially his, as he would say, *'coiffure.'* Obviously, Mr AGDs mind is not on the interview, for this interview takes place in the Graffiti Zone.

AGD feels what can only be described as someone prodding him in the back.

Which, in fact it, was.

'Your cabs here, Mr AGD,' says the receptionist, who has now started to poke him in the chest. 'We've put the change on your account,' turning she quickly walks away suppressing a giggle.

Shaking himself awake, AGD tries to look into the mirror, instead he focuses on someone standing in front of it. Julien stands there, with arms crossed, in one hand he holds a pair of scissors, in the other a comb. He steps aside, points into the mirror, and says, 'Viola.'

AGD looks into the mirror, he blinks, refocuses, blinks again. 'What the..!' He starts to say, only to be interrupted by Julian.

'What indeed,' says Julien, 'for a man of your standing only the best will do. I call this creation the '*AGDd*'. It is retro, iconic and makes a statement about who you are.'

AGD is aghast, 'It, it's, a, a fucking mullet. Last time I saw one of these was during the 70s...do you realise I'm on television in 45 minutes. Getting out of the chair, he is handed a mirror by a smiling Julien, unable to resist checking his hair out, he lets out a scream at what he sees at the back of his head. 'You! You! You butcher. A fucking mullet!' AGD is apoplectic, 'Your...'

'Your cut,' says Julien, 'will set a new trend. The *AGDd* will be on everyone's lips and on their heads. It is council estate chic, a fight on the terraces, a rainy Sunday afternoon walk with a pram-faced girl friend to the local cemetery to kick over gravestones and perhaps cop a feel behind the skip containing dead flowers. It is black and white nostalgia. I will be famous for creating the *AGDd*, and you will be renowned for wearing my creation.

AGD, eyes wide like an animal in a spotlight, looks at Julien, whispers to himself, 'A fucking mullet,' and, unusually for him, considers what Dave the Boulevardier would do. 'Probably go for his throat,' he thinks. Standing tall and looking past Julien he views himself in the mirror. But, I rise above all that, the feelings, the passion. I have cold, hard, objective opinions to impart about about the state of art and what I think it should be.

'You're on the clock Mr AGD, interrupts the cabbie. 'We need to go now if we're to get to the studio in time.'

Throwing a nasty look at Julien, AGD follows the cabbie out of the salon.

Twenty minutes later...

AGD, having been dusted to eliminate forehead shine, is ready for his close-up.

Mariella has given herself hiccups, caused by suppressed giggling.

'We're just waiting for...' Says the studio director, '...in fact, here they are now!'

AGD looks up and clocks Dave and Steve being seated and miked, the studio director points to Mariella saying, 'We're a hairs breath from going live, in 3, 2, 1 and ...

There occurs a simultaneous outburst of laughter, giggling and downright guffawing. Mariella, ever the professional, suppresses a laugh, swallows a hiccup and says...

'Welcome. Tonight we have with us, artists, Dave the London Boulevardier, Steve McCracken famed for his street art of giant, multi-coloured birds, and art critic AGD, who is not known for his love of street art, preferring the term Vandalism. Let's start with AGD, a bad hair day for street art or a renaissance?'

AGD coughs.

'I don't know why I said that,' says Mariella. 'Let me ask you is street art evolving from political comment, and tagging, to fine art? Or is it devolving, returning to what many, including yourself describe as property damage and much like the *'mullet'* you're promoting, becoming less an iconic statement, more a return to the football terraces circa 1973?

AGD bangs his water glass down, 'I didn't come here to be ridiculed.'

'Where do you usually go?' Queries Steve.

'I'll have you know,' spits AGD, 'that my new coiffure is a design classic that begs a revival.'

'It begs for an industrial strimmer,' I suggest, 'let's ask the audience?'

Seven

Portrait of an artista. Name. Wanksta©. Occupation. Graffiti artist. Tonight Mr Wanksta© is going to be in the audience for the week's roundup of the arts. AGD doesn't know it, but he will soon realise, that he and the audience are in the Graffiti Zone.

Mariella, pointing, says, 'Yes. The man with his hand up waving a spray-can...'

'Hi, my name's Wanksta© and I'm a street artist. Graffiti has a long history, from political protest and social comment to tagging, which one can suggest is an existential statement about the individuals sense of self.'

I notice AGD nodding sagely.

'My question,' continues Wanksta©, 'is this. Do want me to put a contract out on the butcher who, and I say this in all seriousness, laughingly cut your hair?'

AGD splutters unable to reply.

Mariella points to another member of the audience, saying, with an obvious attempt to avoid smirking, 'Moving on...'

'My names Suzi Uzi© and I'm a street artist. My question is with Comic Relief coming up, AGD going for the laughs with the mullet to raise money is something we should be applauding, not ridiculing.'

The audience not unfamiliar with irony, applauds wildly, Mariella recognising the futility of trying to keep control, goes with the flow.

'Have you a comment AGD!'

AGD, red faced, explodes shouting, 'My coiffure is not the issue on the table.'

'I beg to differ,' says Wanksta©, your barnet is definitely the issue. Have you considered a new style, perhaps a suede head look, or a flat top?'

'No!'

'What about alopecia?'

AGD rips off his microphone, trips over the cable and with what remains of his dignity storms out of the studio, but not before, to the audiences amusement, stopping in front of a production assistant and using her aluminium clip board as a mirror, checks his hair, and with a flick continues on his way.

'And it's good night from him,' says Mariella.

'Hair today. Gone tomorrow!' Says Wanksta© sporting a cheesy grin.

The audience groan, the studio director winds it up.

'Boys!' I say. 'Why don't we end the night with a Random Act of Mass Hysteria?'

Steve grins…

'But before that we require vast amounts of London Pride.'

Steve grins again, 'A good suggestion well made, let us away...'

Eight

Jon and Joan Johns, average young Londoners who attended a party in Crystal Palace, and on the way home took a detour and found themselves in Hoxton. Most of us on waking in the morning know exactly where we are; the sirens, or the alarm clock brings us out of sleep into the familiar sights, aromas of home and the comfort of a routine day ahead. Not so with our young friends. This will be a day like none they've ever spent – and they'll spend it in the Graffiti Zone.

'J?'

'Yes J.'

'We're not going to find this, *'Best Furniture Store outside of Sweden,'* let's go home.'

'The bible of design is open to interpretation J perhaps we're a little early for the opening.'

'Wallpaper,' is never wrong J it is infallible. We have, perhaps, jumped the gun.'

'I think you're right J. But before we give up let's see where this alley leads to, I can hear music and people laughing.'

Jon and Joan entry the covered alley, lighting the way with their matching Galaxy Class Galaxies, 'God knows where this is leading to,' says J.'

'There's no turning back now,' says J.

J, turning to look realises that there are 20 or 30 people following them, and they'd not get out the way they'd entered.

'This is not like following the walkways at IKEA, 'comments J.

'IKEA!' sighs J, 'I believe our regular attendance at the church of IKEA this Sunday is required.'

'We must pray to the Holy Trinity!'

'Yes indeed, *Habitat, IKEA,* and *Tom Dixon,*' says J.

'Our Holy Trinity!' Proclaims J.

'Oh J!' Says J. 'You are so funny.'

'Thank you J. You too make me smile.'

The couple start to giggle, which begins to escalate into maniacal laughter. 'Where are we? I want to be home, in our matching Norwegian designed PJs J. Snuggled up on the *Ekebol Sofa* watching a box set of Wallander...'

'Discussing the merits, or lack thereof, of the Brannagh version.'

'Oh J.'

'Don't be blue J. Let's go this way.'

Reaching the end of the alley, J and J find themselves in an enclosed courtyard, looking up they clock the giant murals on the windowless walls. There is the sound of spray-cans being shaken and the hiss of paint as it hits the walls, giving Donald Trump a patina the colour of cheesy *Whatsits,* which as it runs down his face eats his skin away revealing a silver terminator skull. J and Js bubbling mania gives way to outright hysteria.

The writing on the wall reads:

'Welcome to a Random Act of Mass Hysteria!'

J holding J tightly, says, 'I don't think we're in Kansas anymore!'

Wanksta© covered in orange paint taps J and J on their shoulders, leaving an orange fingerprint, and says, 'Don't you mean Korea?

J and J in an inadvertent nod to Munch clutch their faces and start to scream, 'Aaarrrh!'

Nine

Picture, if you will, the Daily Mail in a seven page exposé denouncing the perpetrators of the Hoxton murals as, *'Anti-American, Anti-corporate imperialism* and disciples *of the Anti-Christ.*

Picture, if you will, an editorial praising Donald Trump as the greatest American president since Charlie Manson.

There is a sign up ahead, and even though it has been painted over many times, if you look closely enough, you will see it is pointing directly to the Graffiti Zone.

'Aaarrrh! I love the smell of spray-can propellant in the morning,' says Steve.

'*Dum, dum, dum! Dum, dum, dum!*' Hums Vincenzo.

'Why the ominous humming?' I ask.

'We are doomed! I hear the, how you say, galloping of the four horsemen.'

Alan, Putting down his London Pride, says, 'What horsemen Vincenzo?'

'The four horsemen of the Apocalypse. *Dum, dum, dum,*' says Vincenzo swallowing hard.

'Er?!!'

'What?'

'Would you care to explain?' Asks Steve.

'*Dum,dum, dum. Dum, dum, dum,* no one would have believed, in the last days of the summer, that graffiti artists were being watched from CCTV cameras mounted on every available building.'

'I think, in fact, we do believe,' I say, however, what is more pressing is why are you channeling Richard Burton?'

'*Dum, dum, dum,* no one could have dreamed we were being scrutinised by the Old Bill, spurred on by the vitriol of the Daily Mail. Few street artists considered the possibility that there was a plot afoot, and that the Old Bill were drawing-up their plans against us. At midnight on the twelfth of August operation *Anti-Graffiti* was initiated. First will come a raid on the graffiti artists and skateboarders at the South Bank Centre.'

A spokesperson for Banksy said, 'The chances of anything coming from the Met are a million to one,' he said. 'The chances of anything coming from the Met are a million to one-but still they'll come!'

'And,' continues Vincenzo with even more timbre in his voice, 'that's how it will be for the next week, contingents of Old Bill, encouraged by the Daily Mail, which in editorial after editorial will urge it's readership of opinionated mouthfrothers, to grass-up their children, friends, even themselves in the name of all that is, *'Good, Honest and essentially English.'*

The Guardian voiced the liberal agenda and were insistent that the chances of anything coming from this are a million to one,' they said. 'The chances of anything coming from this are a million to one-but still they'll come.'

And they did.

However…

It seems totally incredible that anyone took it seriously. The backlash from the Judiciary focused on the waste of court time, and that the system was overloaded with minor offences and that it wasn't in the public interest to pursue, what the majority of people believe is legitimate artistic expression.

As quickly as it started, it was over, like a 24 hour virus. The Daily Mail claimed victory and moved on to highlight the exodus of people from north of Watford that were invading the South of England and draining it dry of resources, many of these people spoke with regional accents claimed the Daily Express...

'My God,' I say, 'bored, so terribly, terribly bored.' Handing Barry the barman two perfectly folded £50 notes, I take my leave and exit through the bathroom window. As I turn down Winchester Walk, Alan steps out of the shadows of an alley, like the shade of Jack the Ripper.

'Dave.'

'Alan.'

'Dave.'

'Yes Alan?'

'Don't you think this is a little spooky?'

'No!'

'Do you want to feel my shiny, shiny surgical knife?'

'Alan what the fuck are you talking about?'

'I don't know. I have no idea why I was thinking that.'

'Thinking what?'

'That I feel like breakfasting on a plate of sweetbreads, that should put a spring in my step!'

'I still have no idea what you are talking about.'

'That fucking Walter Sickert with his *I'm all right Jack* attitude.

'He's dead.'

'I'm dead?'

'No Alan, Walter Sickert's dead.'

'Oh!'

'What do you want Alan?'

'Breaking news Dave. The Vlad Smythz *From Hell* tour starts tomorrow with a *'pop-up'* comedy concert in the Soho Theatre.'

'Where it all started. Scalp me some tickets Alan. Scalp them now!'

Ten

This is Mr Vlad Smythz, a former dictator of an obscure Eastern European country. Mr Smythz is awaiting trial at The Hague for War Crimes. And where some men leave a mark of their lives as a record of their fragmentary existence on Earth, this man leaves a stain, a bloody viscous, indelible mark to document an evil, despotic sojourn amongst his betters. What you are about to witness is combat between a fascist dictator and an artist, for in just a moment Mr Vlad Smythz, whose life has been given over to absolute totalitarian control, will find his most formidable opponent in the audience, that in reality is on the outskirts of the Graffiti Zone.

'They let you in?' Queries Nine Mil Phil©.

'I thought Deviant Vivika Productions had banned you from attending any and all concerts organised by them.' Says Steve.

'Alan and I, have our ways,' I say, 'it's an old Samurai warrior technique hiding in plain site.'

'In the bar of the Soho Theatre?'

'Where else?'

There is a white, blinding flash of light, as if a spotlight had been turned on. 'Hi, I'm Brad Powers,' says Brad Powers.

'I'm Steve,' says Steve. I believe you're in charge of Public Relations for DVP.

Brad again flashes a smile and his teeth create a supernova effect which dazzles the bar staff into reaching for their Ray Bans.

'Pippa,' says Brad, let's not waste all that private education, be a dear and check if Mr McCracken is on the banned list?'

'Not that you can do anything about it,' says Clive, strolling into the bar.

'You got me,' admits Brad, most people are usually dissuaded from checking the legality of it.' Again he flashes a smile. 'Anyway enjoy the performance.' Turning he exits the bar followed by his entourage of Public Relations Executives, all telling each other what they wanted to hear.

'Let's rock and roll,' says Nine Mil Phil©.

As we leave the Bar, I nod surreptitiously to a guy drinking two large gin and tonics, standing by himself at the bar, 'Actor Cliff Chapman is in the theatre!' I think.

Taking our seats, Alan coughs to get our attention and points to a Sky News Crew setting up at the front of the stage. Political reporter Tim was being mic'd up and sound checked.

'This is a recipe from the Situationalist cookbook,' I say.

'I do hope so,' says Wanksta©.

A spotlight hits a solitary figure on the stage, lighting up his white suit. 'Good evening, I, Lucifer am your MC for this evening, and what an evening it's going to be. Fresh from his audience with Donald Trump, where he outlined a totalitarian strategy for Donald's dictatorship and eventual world domination,' I, Lucifer pauses, looking out to the audience, he says, ' That can't be right, I'll read that again.' Looking up from his notes he shakes his head, 'Well, it's no doubt in the detail. The notes are correct, and whilst I take some time to ponder this, I think it's time to get on with the show, for one night only, welcome to the stage Former Dictator, Vlad Smythz.

The lights go on and Vlad is led to the stage in ankle chains by eight armed guards wearing uniforms of the Pontifical Swiss Guard.

Making his way to the centre of the stage, he clicks his heels together and straight arm salutes the audience. 'I have conquered the stage, and as I said to the Don, we will conquer all the world. You know what he said to me? Of course you don't, that is why you are expendable on my way to world domination. I will tell you, he said nothing, because his reply was too important for spoken words. He smiled a smile of a psychopath who has spent all his life in an asylum for the criminally insane who keeps himself occupied by drawing pictures of flies in crayon and then tearing the wings off and eating the paper. The smile of a lunatic who knows his time is now. And, as is his want, he Tweeted his response, 'Hell Yes Vlad!' I ask the question and I answer it, do you losers realise that your so-called freedom is coming to an end? Why do I, Vlad Smythz, care. The Don and I will rule. There was only one item on our agenda. Total World Domination. But enough about me. Let's talk about the new dictator of the once free world. Ha! I'm still talking about me. Laugh, I goose-step over your cynical smirks. Anyway on with the show, did you hear the one about the Liberal

Democrats and the softly spoken, I could go on but I bore myself with explanations, be that as it may, let me tell you all, these people will go camping. Concentration camping!'

The audience tut and groan, and as as a number of the affronted leave, I clock Cliff with a large G+T in each hand slide into a front row seat.

Vlad salutes the audience and shouts out, 'You people! Yes! You leaving, scared I offend your delicate sensibilities. In my country you would be shot as deserters.'

'*Umm dessert!*'

Vlad startled, looks around, 'Who said that? I demand to know! Have you no respect for a man of my reputation. I could squash you like ants...'

'*Or fly by the seat of my pants, or even have several wanks...*'

The audience are now starting to enjoy the show. Vlad is not enjoying it. He is livid. Pointing to the audience, he snarls, 'You would be up against a wall in a flash!'

'*Flash! Ahh, ahh!*'

'Who said that?'

'Ahh, ahh! The saviour of the universe.'

'You will not escape my retribution, you will hunted down like dogs...'

'He'll save everyone of us.'

The audience start applauding, Alan leans over and whispers, 'It's your mate Cliff isn't it?'

'You are not wrong,' I say.

On stage Vlad is stu, stu,stuttering with anger. 'I, I, I, will hunt...'

'Cunt.'

'I will call on my friend Don Trump...'

'Cunt!'

'You think this is funny...'

'Fanny?'

'The audience can't stop laughing. Vlad shouts to his guards, 'Shoot them, shoot them all!'

'They're having a ball...'

'Vlad grabs his chest looks to the audience and...

'Is this the end my friend?'

The audience have begun to realise there is a ventriloquist in their midst. Vlad, meanwhile, is slowly sinking to his knees, croaking, 'Defibrillator! Get me a def…'

'Knock, knock, knocking on heavens door!'

His armed escort, talking amongst themselves, appear unsure of what to do.

Tim eyeing a scoop, talks to camera, 'In what has been an extraordinary evening, despot Vlad Smythz, awaiting trial at The Hague for war crimes and currently on tour as a stand up comedian, appears to have suffered a heart attack on stage and died. As the world rejoices, I ask members of the audience for there reactions.'

A spotlight picks out I, Lucifer standing over Vlad. Hours later Suzi Uzi will swear she heard him whisper, We can't have this, he hasn't suffered enough on this plane of existence. The spotlight dies and Vlad lives. Getting to his feet Vlad brushes himself off, straight arm salutes the audience, saying, 'Did you think a series of heart attacks could stop my pursuit of world domination?'

'We did hope so!'

Vlad looks at the bottle of water in his hand. 'Why is this bottle talking to me?'

'I'm not! It's the stool!'

'What's the stool?' Says Vlad.

'Clearly insane, Vlad Smythz believes an empty bottle and a stool are talking to him,' approaching Vlad, Tim continues, 'In a Sky News exclusive we were able to film Former Dictator Vlad Smythz survive a heart attack only to lose what was left of his mind...'

'Nurse!' says Vlad

(Kenneth Williams, says Alan)

'And there we have it! Conclusive proof that Vlad Smythz is clinically fucking loony tunes...'

(Brian Blessed says Ms Metro)

'Cliff's best,' I say.

'Who do you think you are?' Screams Vlad.

Tim is unsure, and then appears to say, *'I am Brian the Blessed! I'm making a list. And I'm checking it twice.*

Vlad lunges at Tim.

Tim steps aside.

Vlad is a big man and goes down hard.

Tim is agile.

Vlad struggles to get up.

Tim leaps into the air and scissor kicks Vlad to the head.

Vlad goes down again.

Tim looks to camera and says, 'Now that's what I call breaking news.'

Brad Powers PR Supremo steps in front of Tim and says, 'Do you know who I am?'

Tim, undaunted, says, 'No fucking idea.'

'I'm B...' Brad doesn't get to finish his sentence as Tim punches him in the solar plexus. Brad falls to his knees gasping for air.

Tim adopts the position of the Trafalgar Square pigeon and kicks Brad into Vlad. 'Sometimes,' he says, looking into camera, if the news isn't to your liking, make your own news! I've been...'

'Brian.The Blessed!'

'Cliff's on a roll,' says Alan.

'2 ½ litres of G+T has obviously helped,' I say, as Vlad regains consciousness.

'I'm alive, alive,' Vlad appears to say.

Vlad attempting to get up is finding it difficult as Brad is lying across him. *'I'm alive, and there's a man on top of me. Am I homo-sexual? Oh! Get me Duckie.'*

The audience applaud loudly. Vlad shouts out, 'What are you imbeciles laughing and applauding for? I will see you buried in shallow graves!'

'But not before I've experienced the love of a man. Come on big boy get it on, I want to embrace the life of the softly spoken.'

Vlad is apoplectic, 'I will see you all executed, you will not receive a blindfold, you will not have a last cigarette.'

'But I will kiss you all on the lips...'

This is impressive, he's drinking a gin and tonic and projecting his voice simultaneously,' says Clive.

Vlad struggles to his feet, cries out through lips white with foam, I will kill you all slowly as you gasp for that last cigarette!'

The voice of Brian Blessed booms out, 'But Vlad I vape!'

'I will save you!'

'Who?' asks Vlad.

Flash.'

'Who,' reiterates Vlad.

'Flash.'

'Flash? Says Vlad.

'Ahh, ahh, the saviour of the universe. He'll save everyone of us.'

Vlad loses what's left of his sanity and throws himself into the audience. The audience not wanting to crowd surf the motherfucker step aside, and Vlad hits the floor with a thud.

'He's not getting up from that,' says Alan.

As the guards carry Brad and Vlad out of the theatre, Cliff drinks the last of his gin and tonic and says, *'Tha, tha, that's all folks!'*

Eleven

Witness, if you will, the disinformation perpetrated by the tabloid press that will ensure that Mr and Mrs Average Citizen will sit up and take notice. They will also, given enough rope, form a mob and take to the streets carrying flaming torches, and with this rope they will lynch whomever the Daily Mail blame for their current woes. But there are also those who will oppose the manipulation and scapegoating they too will take to the streets and boulevards with spray-cans, for as Dave the Boulevardier is much quoted as saying, 'Whatever the Daily Mail disapprove of, I'll wholeheartedly embrace.' There is a signpost up-ahead and it is pointing to fair and balanced reporting and it leads to the Graffiti Zone.

The Daily Mail in a front page exclusive claim to have proof that the Holy See were not involved in the Vlad Smythz debacle. Although as a contribution to World peace they did supply a cadre of Vatican guards to ensure his safety and the safety of others. A spokesperson for the Pope said, *'We remain neutral we do not support fascist dictatorships, however, until the International War Crimes Commission has made it's decision, we the Holy Catholic Church will ensure fair-play and it is to this end we shall provide Vlad Smythz with protection, he is innocent until proven guilty.'* The spokesperson went on to say, *'In the interests of full disclosure, the Office of the Vatican acknowledge as true, reports that Deviant Vivika Productions (DVP) its Public Relations Department, and its VP Brad Powers are, the sole provider of PR for the Vatican. Our relationship with DVP and Mr Powers is longstanding, we can confirm that the Pontiff was unaware of this as he is shielded from the mundanities of everyday business affairs to allow him the time to concentrate on more spiritual matters. Which is why he, initially, denied all knowledge of this, what has been described, perhaps correctly, symbiotic relationship. Furthermore, his Holiness's comments that DVP was little more than an agent of Satan was inappropriately and incorrectly reported and accordingly the Vatican Council has stricken these comments from the records. I now take this opportunity to confirm that the Pontiff did not say the words that were attributed to him. Subsequent to this, I can confirm that DVP and its subsidiary DVP PR and its VP Brad Powers have our upmost confidence and we will continue to have a professional relationship with them.'*

'Well, 'I say, ' I'm all broken-up about Vlad Smythz and his human rights.'

'I echo that statement,' says Nine Mil Phil©.

'And I Clive,' says Clive, 'will fund the counterattack.'

'And I, as representative of the Russian Cultural Institute,' says Ivanka, strolling into the Rake, will provide resources to the artists to enable this power-play to materialise.'

'Darling,' I say, 'this is good timing.'

'Da Dave, I came by submarine.'

'Er why?'

'By Putin's sputum comrade, just to prove we can!'

'Is that a wetsuit, 'queries Wanksta©.

'You flatter me comrade, it is new improvement on inferior Western latex.'

'It doesn't reflect the light,' says Suzi Uzi©.

'It is designed for stealth, Dave requires challenge comrade.'

'It fits so snugly,' says Ms Metro, 'how do you take it off?'

'There is only one way to remove this garment comrade.'

'Pray tell,' I say, already knowing the answer, but loving the twinkle in Ivanka's eye and the knowing smile.

'This garment can only be removed by spanky-lashing it off. I recommend 50 lashes to start comrade.'

'That's answered the question,' says Ms Metro, looking a little flushed.

'Comrade Dave.'

'Yes Ivanka.'

'By Lenin's waxy dome, the garment must be removed.'

'When?'

'As soon as possible, comrade Dave, I go back to studio now, you will find me lying across sofa. I know you will not be long.

'How so Ivanka?'

'Because comrade, if 50 lashes does not remove this Matt Black, light absorbing garment, I recommend 25 strokes with the spanky-stick, which I will get out for you.'

'Say no more,' I say.

'Da comrade Dave, I will not. However, I expect you will want me to count out the strokes.'

'Yes Ivanka,' I say, 'indeed I will.'

'Dave.'

'Ivanka.'

'Dave.'

'Yes Ivanka.'

'I go now comrade. I suggest you terminate this conclave of creatives with prejudice and exit through the bathroom window.'

'This meeting is…'I begin to say.

'…over?' Says Wanksta©.

'…fini?' Contributes Vincenzo.

'…adjourned?' Suggests Clive.

'…closed?' Queries Colin 45©.

'I believe, it's now academic as Dave has exited through the loo window,' says Alan.

Twelve

Showery summer evening, the present. Order of events, the opening reception of the *Street Art is* News exhibition. Representatives of the Gallery and the Russian Cultural Institute, co-funders of the exhibition, are talking with the artists before the show opens in precisely 5 minutes. The so-called free press have failed to RSVP. However, this will not stop them writing editorials condemning the show. On the pavement are AGD and his film crew, hoping to complete the documentary on Dave, the London Boulevardier. Dave has agreed to be interviewed by AGD on behalf of the Gallery. His contribution to the show, three canvases, the subject his girlfriend Ivanka. As the clock edges its way towards 8pm, the principals in question will find themselves on the threshold of the Graffiti Zone.

AGD looks into the window of the Gallery and in one sweeping movement tousles his hair, says to his reflection, 'Because I'm worth it,' winks at himself, and turning to face the camera, continues, 'Dave what surprises have you in store for us this evening.'

'That's an interesting question!'

'Thank you Dave. Can you give us an example, without giving too much away.'

'Yes I can.'

'Thanks Dave. So, what are we in for?'

'An experience.'

'Will you describe this experience?'

'Yes.'

AGD swallows, shouts 'Cut,' and walks over to a lamppost with a laminated photograph cable-tied to it. Taking a deep breath, he counts to ten, breathes out, and looking at his reflection in the photograph, flicks his hair, shouts, 'Rolling and Action.' Turning to camera, he winks at the camera operator saying, 'Yes, I know what you're thinking, 'It's because he's worth it.'

'No, I wasn't,' says the camera guy, I was thinking, 'What a   wanker!'

AGD pauses, thinks, fails to extemporise a response, notices that Dave has re-entered the Gallery. Pointing at the camera crew, he says, 'Follow me.' Striding into the Gallery, he thinks he hears a faint ,'Fuck you!'

The camera guy has gathered the crew around the lamppost. 'Look at this,' he says indicating the laminated photograph. 'We can get a documentary out of this, Channel 5 would love it!' The photograph,' he says, is of a black cat, named Tiddles, and apparently was last seen on Sunday morning. There is a reward offered, and a contact telephone number. However, what is interesting are these post-it notes running all the way down the lamppost.

The first yellow post-it says, *'We have your cat. It will cost you to see him again.'*

The second pink post-it asks, *'How much to get Tiddles back?'*

Post-it 3 asks, *'How much you got?'*

Post-it 4 says, *'How much do you want? I love my Tiddles!'*

Post-it 5 says, *'£500 quids.'*

Post-it 6 asks, *Where shall I leave it?'*

Post-it 7 says, 'On the pavement by this lamppost.'

Post-it 8 says, 'It might get stolen.'

Post-it 9 says, 'Who would want to steal 500 pounds of squid?'

Post-it 10 says, 'What are you talking about?'

Post-it 11 says, 'Squids.'

Post-it 12 says, 'I thought you wanted cash.'

Post-it 13 says, 'Cash. Don't fuck with us. We want squids or octopus.'

Post-it 14 says, 'I want to see proof of life.'

Post-it 15 says, 'If I'm writing these post-its I must be alive.'

Post-it 16 says, 'Not you, my cat Tiddles.'

Post-it 17 says, 'Can't do that.'

Post-it 18 says, 'Why not?'

Post-it 19 says, 'We've eaten him.'

Post-it 20 says, 'Why oh why.'

Post-it 21 says, 'We ran out of squid.'

Post-it 22 says, 'You won't get any now.'

Post-it 23 says, 'And you won't get Charlie back.'

Post-it 24 says, *'You've stolen Charlie?'*

Post-it 25 says, *'You shouldn't have tied him to the lamppost.'*

Post-it 26 says, *'How much to return Charlie?'*

Post-it 27 says, *'750 of your seaside deckchairs.'*

Post-it 28 says, *'Do you mean shekels?'*

Post-it 29 says, *'No mussels.'*

'And that's where it ends.'

'Where's Alan,' queries Wanksta©.

'In the back of that white van filming his latest found sculpture piece.'

'The one with Post-it notes?'

'Yep! I think Channel 5 are interested.'

'DAVE.'

'Yes.'

'We need to talk about my documentary.'

'You may. I don't. I have other things on my mind.'

'Such as?'

'Well since you ask, my next flower arranging class, we're going to create the *Last Supper* in a selection of tulips, daisies, lilac and assorted flowering shrubs.'

'You jest Dave.'

'And you wound me.' I say.

'I...' says AGD stopping suddenly as his eye catches a glimpse of himself staring out of a canvas. 'I, I, I. They're all of me. Why are they all of me?'

'We're living in a new age, the *Age of the Selfie.* And you have always been at the cutting edge of the self-obsessed.'

'It's because I'm worth it.'

'And there we have it.' I say.

There is a cry of 'Outstanding,' followed by 'Brilliant,' and 'These are Dave's best works yet!'

AGD heads toward the excited throng, I, on the other hand, having painted the fuckers head toward the bar. 'Four bottles of London Pride and four bottles of London Pride as chasers my good man.' I say.

'I'm waiting for his reaction,' says Nine Mil Phil©.

There is an almighty, 'Ahh!' Followed by a plaintiff, 'Arrrrrrrrrr!' ending in a mewing, 'Aaaaaaaaaaaaaaaaaaaa!'

There is a shout of 'Medic.'

Vincenzo drinking his Peroni through a straw, exclaims, 'Mother of Mercy, isa this whata you call, *'Man down.'*

The soundtrack, classic hip-hop, circa 70s, segue-ways into the theme from MASH.

AGD is lying on the floor being fanned by a gallery assistant, while Suzi Uzi© kneeling is tightening his tie around his neck.

Meandering over, I say, I could be wrong Suzi, but shouldn't you be loosening his clothing?'

'You're wrong, she replies, pulling tightly on both ends of his tie.

'I tried,' I say, 'Lord knows I tried,' and take one of the ends.

Suzi without breaking concentration, says, 'Thanx Dave. Now pull?'

As we begin to tug on his tie, two green leather enrobed London Ambulance Service medics arrive. 'Thanks guys,' they say, we'll take over now.'

'Drink Dave,' asks Suzi.

'Don't mind if I do,' I say, 'don't mind if I do.'

'We join Alan and the Usual Suspects at the bar, 'I see he viewed your latest,' says Alan and if you don't mind me saying so, as a critic he's falling down on the job.'

'Hello,' says a geezer approaching the bar. 'Sorry I'm late, you know how it is, Underground, taxis, distressed art critics...'

Smiling broadly he proffers his hand, I'm Sebastian from the Guardian Kulcha section, I'm here to review the show.'

'Be our guest,' I say, 'be our guest.'

'Comrade!'

'Yes Ivanka.'

'Who is this smiling man?'

'Sebastian meet Ivanka. Ivanka meet Sebastian.'

'A round of London Pride on the Guardian expense account,' I say.

Thirteen

'Served for your consideration a montage of possibilities. The choices are there for the taking. The outcomes of these choices you will only find out at the end of your journey. The signpost points the way, your destination The Graffiti Zone.

Siting around a table in the Hawksmore, Covent Garden, Alan orders everything on the breakfast menu x3.

'You mean,' queries the waiter-person, 'each of your party will eat everything we have for breakfast three times?'

'Yes,' replies Alan.

'And your Italian friend is going to commandeer the Gaggia machine?'

'Yes,' I say, 'the espressos will flow. Which reminds me ten espresso doppios Vincenzo. Grazia.'

'Si. The crema will be perfecto.'

'I'll have two,' says Alan.

'And me,' says Wanksta©.

'Actually, I'll have two as well,' says Clive.

'Me two, too, I think,' says a slightly perplexed Suzi Uzi©.

'Vincenzo,' says Alan, 'make it twenty espresso doppios.'

'Okay, they are, how you say, onward.'

'On there way,' replies Alan.

'Vincenzo.'

'Si Dave.'

'Vincenzo, I've changed my mind, I'll have three espresso doppios. Grazia.'

'Dave.'

'Vincenzo.'

'Dave.'

'Vincenzo.'

'Dave.'

'Yes Vincenzo.'

'Don't push me!'

Nine Mil Phil© and Colin 45 arrive with the papers.

'Well,' I say, 'there's a copy each, let's see what they have to say.'

'The Daily Mail reports that president Trump, is, in his own words, 'not (expletive deleted) happy' with the *Street Art is* News exhibition, as witnessed by a number of Tweets posted by him. The first Tweet says, 'Who are these Limey mother f******? Who the f*** do they think they are?'

The second Tweet continued in the same vitriolic vein, 'Don't these Limeys realise that if we hadn't won WW2 for them, they'd be eating sauerkraut for every meal. They're as grateful as the garlic eating, Nazi collaborating, shower avoiding frogs. And while I'm on the subject who does Twitter think they are trying to limit how much I can s...'

He continued Tweeting throughout the night, his final Tweet said, 'Do these Limey mother f****** know who I am? I am POTUS, I can bring a hard rain down at the flick of a switch!'

'And on and on he rants,' says Alan.

'Turn to the Guardian,' says Ms Metro.

The front page of the redesigned tabloid format paper, declared, under Sebastian Bell's byline, that, 'Graffiti as a political tool, is just as effective a means for political change as party political broadcasts, editorials or manifestos.

Turner Prize winning *Found Sculpture Artist* Alan, the London Boulevardier, Wanksta©, and many more street artists used graffiti as a weapon to comment on contemporary politics. A character was created for the show, AGD. This logo was sprayed, stencilled and painted by acclaimed Street Artist Steve McCracken. Steve painted his signature style birds sitting on the shoulder of Donald Trump quoting lines from Dirty Harry films. Dave the London Boulevardier using his girlfriend Ivanka, Director of the Russian Cultural

Institute as a model for three outstanding pieces of work. He painted her with portraits of AGD covering all of her naked body.

As a comment on vanity it struck a nerve with one critic, perhaps identifying with it too closely, who shrieked and hit the floor in a dead faint. Allegedly, this critic is also known as AGD. The Boulevardier triptych was titled *Because I'm Worth It!'*

Asked to sum up the impact of the work on show, the Boulevardier commented, 'Artists don't build walls to keep people out, we use walls to engage people. Walls are our canvas. He also said, 'I require the bathroom!' This reporter can confirm that the Boulevardier was not seen for the remainder of the show, having climbed out of the bathroom window.

As a counterpoint to the current political debate it was telling, relevant and darkly satirical.

The exhibition run for the next three weeks.

Fourteen

Presented for your consideration the so-called leader of the free world, Donald Trump, President of the USA. A man ridiculed by the majority of the free world. He has aligned himself with a man who requires little introduction, a man who is loathed by the majority of humankind, Vlad Smythz, former dictator and despot.

This meeting of minds, this meeting of strategic alliances could only happen in the Graffiti Zone.

'Dave!'

'Yes Ms Metro.'

'**Hell.No!** are reporting that Donald Trump is Tweeting about the only politician that understands him.'

'You don't mean!'

'That was not very dramatic Dave.'

'YOU DON'T MEAN!'

'Close.'

'**YOU DON'T MEAN!**'

'Yes Dave I do, Vlad Smythz. Trump is saying that when Vlad's trial is over and the War Crimes Tribunal inevitability return a verdict of not guilty, he expects him to enter the next presidential election as his running mate.'

'I think, perhaps we have other matters to address...you're sitting in a pool of water!'

'I was going to mention that. My waters have broken!'

'I'll get a cab...'

'And Dave, don't let Alan use the placenta as a found sculpture...'

25655947R00069

Printed in Poland
by Amazon Fulfillment
Poland Sp. z o.o., Wrocław